Papa & Gigi's DAY OFF

BY MARY & RICHARD KOZIEL

ILLUSTRATED BY LEIGH HAUER

Suite 300 - 990 Fort St
Victoria, BC, V8V 3K2
Canada

www.friesenpress.com

PapaandGigisadventures.com

ISBN
978-1-5255-7275-3 (Hardcover)
978-1-5255-7276-0 (Paperback)
978-1-5255-7277-7 (eBook)

1. Juvenile Fiction, Family, Multigenerational

Distributed to the trade by The Ingram Book Company

This book is dedicated to our wonderful
children, Jessica and Brandon, and to our
precious grandchildren, Oliver and Eleanor
who inspired us to write this book.

And to our son-in-law, Joe, because if it
were not for him, this book would never have
been finished.

Papa and Gigi have the DAY OFF. Their grandchildren are staying home with their parents today, so Papa and Gigi don't have to babysit.

"We have the DAY OFF!" yells Gigi.

"FINALLY! Let's enjoy our day off together," says Papa.

"I know what we can do," Gigi says. "Let's make breakfast at home today."

"WHAT A GOOD IDEA,"
says Papa.

"This will be FUN," Gigi says.

OH NO! Gigi's breakfast is
on fire!

"I set the eggs on fire!" cries
Gigi. "I forgot to flip the eggs.
Breakfast is ruined."

"I'll put it out, Gigi,"
Papa says.

"IT'S OKAY," Papa says. "I wasn't hungry anyway. Let's do something else."

"I know what we can do," says Gigi. "Let's go get our hair done!"

"WHAT A GOOD IDEA," says Papa.

"This will be FUN," Gigi says.

Gigi and Papa are at the hairdresser's.

"Just cut a LITTLE off the top," Papa tells the hairdresser.

"Please make my hair nice and wavy," Gigi says with a big smile.

The hairdresser is all done cutting their hair, but something is not right.

"OH NO! She shaved all of my hair off!" Papa yells. "I just wanted a little off the top!"

Gigi cries, "My hair is not wavy—it's CRAZY!"

"THAT'S OKAY," Papa says. "You still look great. Let's do something else."

"I know what we can do," says Gigi. "Let's go to the gym!"

"WHAT A GOOD IDEA," says Papa.

"This will be FUN," Gigi says.

Gigi and Papa are at the gym.

Gigi says to Papa, "Please be careful lifting those weights, Papa."

"DON'T WORRY, GIGI," Papa says. "They are not too heavy for me. But make sure you don't ride too fast on that bicycle."

"DON'T BE SILLY, PAPA," Gigi answers.

OH NO! Papa has dropped the weights on his foot, and Gigi is about to take off like a rocket ship to the moon.

"MY TOE, MY TOE!" yells Papa. "Those weights were too heavy for me."

"SOMEONE STOP ME!" Gigi screams. "I'm pedaling too fast!"

"Don't worry Gigi! I'll SAVE you," says Papa.

"THAT'S OKAY," Papa says. "I was too tired to exercise anyway. Let's do something else."

"I know what we can do," says Gigi. "Let's go on a picnic!"

"WHAT A GOOD IDEA," says Papa.

"This will be FUN," Gigi says.

Gigi and Papa have their picnic all set up.

Gigi asks Papa, "You don't think we are too close to the tree, do you? I don't want any bugs to fall on me."

"Oh, not at all," Papa says. "What could POSSIBLY go wrong here?"

"You're right; it's perfect," says Gigi. "It is a great day for a picnic."

Papa and Gigi are about to enjoy their picnic when...

"OH NO! OH NO!" Gigi shrieks. "There are a bunch of ants taking away our food!"

"And look," Papa says. "There's a bird flying off with our basket and a squirrel eating our food," he says.

"They've TAKEN our picnic!" Gigi cries.

"THAT'S OKAY," Papa says. "It was getting too hot to eat outside anyway. Let's do something else."

"I know what we can do," says Gigi. "Let's go for a long drive."

"WHAT A GOOD IDEA," says Papa.

"This will be FUN," Gigi says.

Papa and Gigi are driving along in their car.

Gigi asks Papa, "Did you check the engine before we left, Papa?"

"Of COURSE I did," Papa says. "Everything is fine. What can go wrong here?"

"PERFECT," says Gigi. "It is a great day for a car ride."

OH NO! Something is wrong with Papa and Gigi's car.

"There is SMOKE coming out of the engine!" Papa yells.

"And look, Papa," Gigi cries. "There is a flat tire back here. Our car ride is RUINED."

"THAT'S OKAY," Papa says. "I was getting tired of sitting so long. After I call for a tow truck, let's do something else."

"I know what we can do," says Gigi. "Let's walk home."

"WHAT A GOOD IDEA," says Papa.

"This will be FUN," Gigi says.

Gigi and Papa are walking
down the road.

"Just you and me going
for a walk, Gigi," Papa
says. "Nothing can go
wrong here."

"I KNOW," Gigi says.
"It's so quiet and sunny.
It's perfect. It is a great
day for a walk."

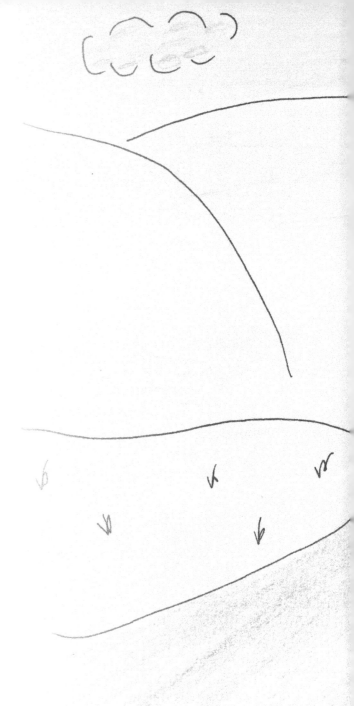

OH NO! Papa and Gigi are caught in a storm.

"Oh man!" Papa yells. "Can you believe this? And we are still quite a way from home. We are going to have to hurry up."

"I know," Gigi moans. "Our walk is RUINED! And it was such a sunny day today."

Papa and Gigi are back at their house now.

"This is NOT okay," Papa says quietly. "Everything we tried to do today was ruined. Let's not do anything else."

"But Papa, I know what we can do," says Gigi.

Gigi whispers something in Papa's ear.

"WHAT A GOOD IDEA," says Papa.

"This will be FUN," Gigi says.

Papa and Gigi
arrive at their
grandchildren's house.

"Can we BABYSIT today?"
Gigi asks with excitement.

"Of course you can!"
everyone on the
porch yells.

"WHAT A GREAT IDEA,"
says Papa.

"This will be FUN,"
Gigi says.

Papa and Gigi have the day off. They get to spend time with their grandchildren today after all.

NOTHING CAN GO WRONG HERE...

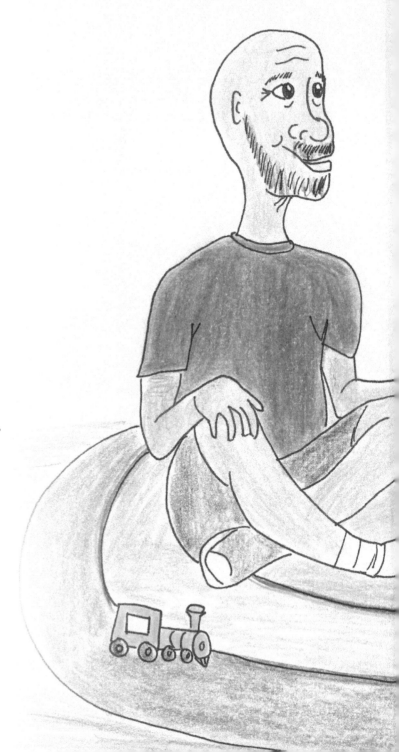

CPSIA information can be obtained
at www.ICGtesting.com
Printed in the USA
JSHW030857030720
6470JS00002B/5

9 781525 572760